Flower
Power

First published in 2014 by Wayland
Text copyright © Wayland 2014
Illustrations © Wayland 2014

Wayland
338 Euston Road
London NW1 3BH

Wayland Australia
Level 17/207 Kent Street
Sydney, NSW 2000

Series Editor: Victoria Brooker
Series design: Robert Walster and Basement68
Consultant: Dee Reid

A CIP catalogue record for this book is available
from the British Library.
Dewey number: 823.9'2-dc23

ISBN 978 0 7502 8226 0
eBook ISBN: 978 0 7502 8566 7

2 4 6 8 10 9 7 5 3 1

Printed in China

Wayland is a division of Hachette Children's Books,
an Hachette UK Company
www.hachette.co.uk

Flower Power

Tom Easton and Sophie Escabasse

WAYLAND
www.waylandbooks.co.uk

Miss Collins is the Careers Officer. She's been fixing up work experience for me.

I was late for the meeting.

Mum put diesel into the car.

It should have been petrol.

All the good jobs were gone
when I arrived.

"Hello, Dan," Miss Collins said.
"There's not much left I'm afraid."

"Are there any jobs at the football club?" I asked. "Or could I be a roadie for a rock band?"

"No," she said. "What about the Rubbish Tip? They need someone to sweep the yard."

"That's not living the dream," I said.

"Is there anything else?" I asked.

"Here you go," Miss Collins said.

I read the card she gave me.

"Working in a flower shop?" I said. "I was hoping for something a bit more...cool."

"You could get quite chilly sweeping the yard at the Rubbish Tip," said Miss Collins.

"OK," I said quickly. "I'll take the job in the flower shop."

The lady at the flower shop was called Jenny. She was very pretty. I found it hard to listen to what she was saying.

"I'll take the orders," she said.
"You deliver the flowers. OK?"
"OK," I said, nodding.

"It's Valentine's Day tomorrow," Jenny said. "So there will be lots of people ordering roses. Make sure you don't..."

14

I wondered whether Jenny had a
boyfriend. If she didn't, maybe she'd
spend Valentine's Day with me?
I would be happy to work late.

"...is that all OK?" she finished.
I nodded, but I hadn't heard
anything she had just said.

In the back room I had an idea.
I hid a rose. It was the best
one there. I would give it to Jenny
on Valentine's Day.

The next day everything went well.

Jenny kept shouting out orders.

"A dozen for Mrs James
at 26 Pitt Street."

"6 long-stems for Miss Cooper
on the High Street."

"Two dozen for Anita at
13 Grove Street."

I would rush out of the back room
carrying boxes. What a lot of roses!
I felt a bit mean only giving
Jenny one rose.

After lunch, we ran out of roses.

"A dozen for Mrs Harrison at..."
Jenny began.

"We've run out," I called back.

There was a pause.

"What?" Jenny called.

"We've run out of roses," I said.
Jenny came into the back room.

"How can we have run out?"
she said. "I bought a thousand."
  "Well they were big orders,"
I explained. "A dozen boxes here,
a dozen boxes there. It all adds up."

"Boxes?" she cried, in horror.
"When I say a dozen, I mean a
dozen roses. Not a dozen boxes!"

I looked around at the empty room.

"Now you tell me," I said.

Jenny sank down onto a chair.

Maybe I could cheer her up.

I took out the rose and gave it to her.

"As there are no more roses,"
I said, "maybe we could close early.
We could go for a nice walk
by the river?"

OK. Maybe I got things a bit wrong...
And maybe it wasn't the best time
to give her the rose.

But did she have to make me eat it?

Read more stories about Dan.

978 0 7502 8228 4

Dan's latest work experience is at a car yard. All Dan has to do is sell a car. What could possibly go wrong?

978 0 7502 8225 3

Dan's latest work experience is as a grave digger. All Dan has to do is dig a hole. What could possibly go wrong?

978 0 7502 8227 7

Dan's latest work experience is at a radio station. All Dan has to do is mop floors. What could possibly go wrong?

Read some more books in the Freestylers series.

FOOTBALL FACTOR

Each story follows the ups
and downs of one member
of the football team Sheldon
Rovers as they aim for
Cup glory.

978 0 7502 7985 7

978 0 7502 7980 2

978 0 7502 7982 6

978 0 7502 7984 0

978 0 7502 7981 9

978 0 7502 7983 3

SHORT THRILLERS

Cool crime detectives, Jas and Sam, solve spine-chilling
cases with humour and bravery.

978 0 7502 6895 0

978 0 7502 6896 7

978 0 7502 6898 1

978 0 7502 6897 4

FOR TEACHERS

About Freestylers

Freestylers is a series of carefully levelled stories, especially geared for struggling readers. With very low reading age and high interest age, these books are humorous, fun, up-to-the-minute and edgy. Core characters provide familiarity in all of the stories, build confidence and ease pupils from one story through to the next, accelerating reading progress.

Freestylers can be used for both guided and independent reading. To make the most of the books you can:

- Focus on making each reading session successful. Talk about the text before the pupil starts reading. Introduce the characters, the storyline and any unfamiliar vocabulary.

- Encourage the pupil to talk about the book during reading and after reading. How would they have felt if they were one of the characters? How would they have dealt with the situations that Dan found himself in?

- Talk about which parts of the story they like best and why.

For guidance, this story has been approximately measured to:

National Curriculum Level: 2C
Reading Age: 6
Book Band: Orange

ATOS: 2.1
Lexile ® Measure [confirmed]: 350L